My Nutty

Grampa!

By Neil Baron

Illustrations by David Garner

DEDICATION

To all my grandchildren who have been
a source of immeasurable joy for me.

1

My name is Owen and my little sister is Lucy,
and we have a nutty grandpa. We call him Censio
because that's what he wants to be called.
Don't ask me why. Maybe it's because he's nutty.

So that's what all his grandchildren call him—

Sometimes when Lucy and I cry, Censio sits next to us and cries with us. But he cries much louder than Lucy and I put together. He just keeps crying and crying louder and louder until Lucy and I start to laugh. Then he gets up and walks away.

Why do you think Censio does this?

Because he's nutty!

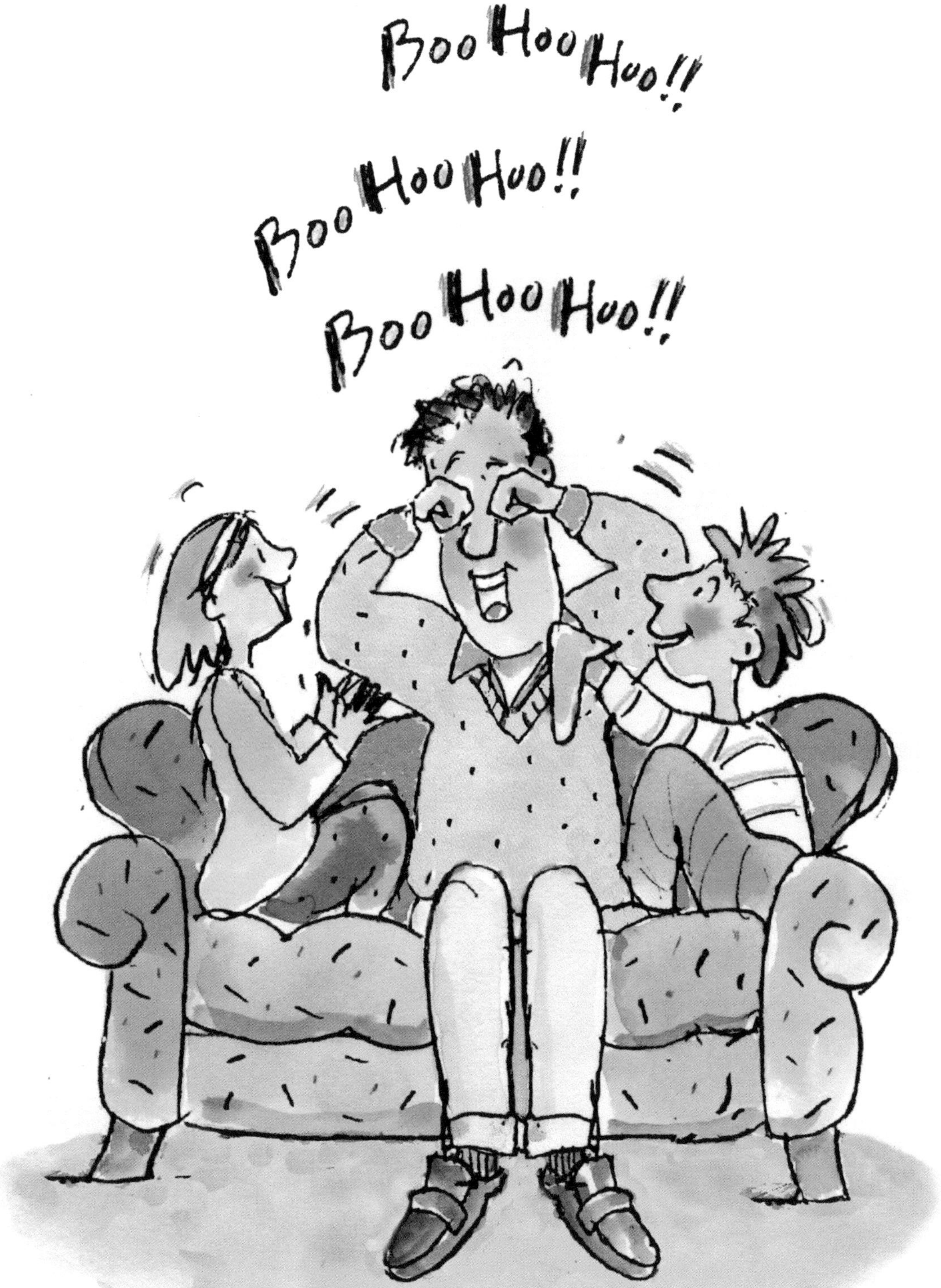
BooHooHuo!!
BooHooHuo!!
BooHooHuo!!

When Censio takes me somewhere in the car, I sit in the back in my car seat. Once Censio got in the back seat with me and said, "Let's go." I said, "Censio, there's no one in the driver's seat." He just kept yelling, "Let's go, let's go!" until I started yelling it with him. It was fun. Finally Censio got in the front and drove.

Why do you think Censio does this?

Because he's nutty!

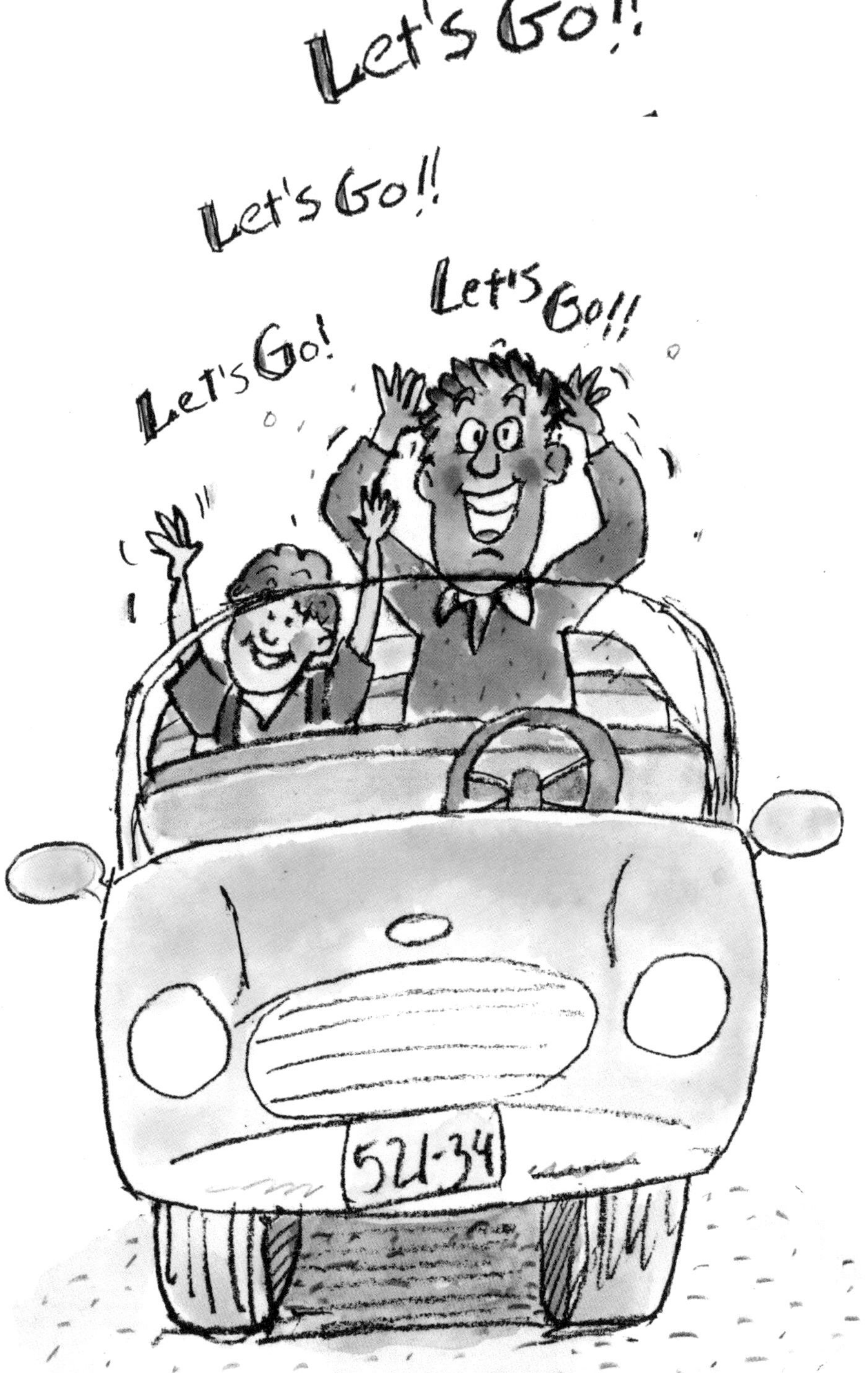
Let's Go!!
Let's Go!!
Let's Go!!
Let's Go!
521-34

Sometimes when a song comes on that Censio likes, he jumps up and does a crazy dance that looks like a tall bird with a broken leg. Then I jump up and do the same dance right behind him. I guess it's because Censio's having so much fun that I want to join in.

Why do you think Censio does this?

Because he's nutty!

Sometimes Censio says he has to do his exercises and will get in the middle of the room and do exercises that I'm sure no one else in the whole world does. They look a lot like the bird dance he does, but he also makes faces that no one else in the whole world would make or would want to make, except me, when I get up and do the same exercises and make the same faces. I don't know why, Censio just makes me want to do it.

Why do you think Censio did this?

Because he's nutty!

Once Censio was driving Lucy, me and Grandma somewhere and playing classical music. Lucy and I said "That's music for old people." What did Censio do? He made it louder and started waving his arms to the music and bouncing up and down. He even hit his head on the ceiling. It looked like so much fun that Lucy and I joined in. We liked the music much more when we did what Censio was doing.

Why do you think Censio did this?

Because he's nutty!

Here's how Censio taught me left from right. When we were walking to a playground, Censio put me on his shoulders, closed his eyes and said, "Now you tell me which way to go, left or right, so I don't walk into a tree or a bush or into the street." When Censio was walking towards the street, I yelled, "left!" so he stayed on the sidewalk. But when he walked towards some bushes, I didn't say anything. You can guess what happened. We both laughed a lot when he walked into the bush. Anyway, that's how I learned left from right.

Why do you think Censio did this?

Because he's nutty!

When Censio reads books to Lucy and me, he likes to make up his own part of the story. Once he was reading a book about two children and their father who get scared by a bear and run away. Censio made up a part where I came into the cave, picked up the bear, put it on my shoulders and spun it around and around until it got dizzy and fell down so it couldn't chase the children and their father. Then Censio read the real story for a while, but then made up a part where Lucy made friends with the bear. He finally finished the story.

Why do you think Censio did this?

Because he's nutty!

Censio has a weird way of sneezing when he reads to us he. First he'll say, "Sneeze coming, sneeze coming." Then he takes several deep breathes, and sneezes very loud and so strong that the sneeze blows the book out of his hands all the way up to the ceiling! When the book falls back down, Censio reads some more until he does the same thing all over again. Censio always finished the book, but it just took longer.

Why do you think Censio does this?

Because he's nutty!

Censio made up this game called "What do You Prefer?" But it isn't what you'd expect. He asked me, "What do you prefer, drinking hot chocolate or eating a tree?" Well, who doesn't know the answer to that one? Then he says, "It's your turn, Owen." And I'd say, "What do you prefer, eating a bagel or falling in a mud puddle?" Censio pretends to be thinking, rubs his chin and says, "That's a tough one; let me think about that one."

Why do you think Censio does this?

Because he's nutty!

When it rains in the summer, Censio waits until dark, and says, "It's frog-grabbing time!" We take a bucket into the car, put on our high beams and drive very slowly. Sure enough, we see some frogs, get out of the car, grab them, put them in the bucket, and bring them home for everyone to see. Usually we let them go. But once we let them loose in the kitchen while Grammy was cooking. That was Censio's idea.

Why do you think Censio does this?

Because he's nutty!

The real reason Censio does these nutty things
is because it makes us laugh
and that makes him happy
'cause he loves us.

25164175R20020

Made in the USA
Charleston, SC
17 December 2013